CRAZY BAD

Laura Shenton

CRAZY BAD

Laura Shenton

Iridescent Toad Publishing

Iridescent Toad Publishing.

Cover by Chan Cover Designs.

First edition. ISBN 978-1-913779-08-5

Chapter One

The neon lights of the eastern city blocks flickered erratically, casting jagged reflections onto the wet asphalt below. A steady drizzle turned the pavement into a mirror, amplifying the garish reds and blues that bled from the signs above. Chesney pulled her hood tighter over her head, the fabric soaked through and dampening her long, pink-streaked blonde hair. She swung the wooden bat in her gloved hand lazily at her side, its varnished surface gleaming with streaks of fluorescent light.

The streets smelt like desperation. Cigarette smoke, sour liquor, and damp concrete clung to the air, making it uncomfortable to breathe deeply. Chesney didn't bother trying. She didn't frequent the city at night to enjoy its finer points – she came to do her job.

Tonight's job wasn't much different from the others, but she was tired of it all. The running. The violence. The never-ending spiral of taking orders from people who thought they owned her. Delgado didn't own her – no one did – but it was easier to keep her head down and play the part than to resist.

Chesney spotted her target at the end of the street. Harper. He immediately tried to duck into a side alley, pulling his hood low and hunching his shoulders, but Chesney was faster. She cut him off, blocking his escape route with a deliberate step that planted her squarely in his path.

"Going somewhere?" she asked, an edge to her voice that made Harper freeze.

"Oh, hey," he said nervously, feebly attempting a smile. "I was just..."

"Save it," Chesney insisted, pressing him against the wall like a cornered animal.

"Please," he begged. "I can explain!"

His lanky frame looked even thinner in the

shadows, his stained hoodie hanging off his shoulders. Chesney didn't care; she didn't feel sorry for him at all. He was just another job, another problem to be dealt with. Her grip on her bat tightened.

"You've got thirty seconds," she said, her voice calm, almost bored.

"I... I just need more time, ok?" he stammered, his mouth moving faster than his brain, his hands moving up defensively. "Things have been tight lately. My girl's sick, and the hospital bills..."

"Twenty seconds," she interrupted.

His face crumpled, a mixture of panic and shame.

"I swear I'll get the money," he said pleadingly. "Just one more week, that's all I'm asking."

"Delgado's expecting full payment," Chesney said, her tone sharp and demanding.

"I know, I know, but I just..."

"But nothing," Chesney interrupted, taking a step closer and tapping the thick end of her bat in her palm. "You owe him, Harper. You don't get to rewrite the rules just because you've had a bad week."

"Yes, I know, but..."

Chesney lifted the bat, pressing it against the wall near Harper's face. She knew she wouldn't need to strike him; this alone was creating enough tension to make him flinch. The varnished wood caught the neon light, a silent threat. As she looked him dead in the eyes, the streetlamp close by made her shadow loom unnaturally large against the alley's walls. Harper's breathing came in short, panicked bursts as he stared at her.

"Here's how this is gonna work," she said, her tone conversational. "You've got three days. Not a week. Three days. If you don't have the cash by then, I won't be as nice about it."

"I'll get it, I swear," Harper said frantically, almost sycophantic. "Three days, no problem."

With a nod of her head, Chesney took a step back and rested her bat on her shoulder. She turned to leave, but something stopped her. Out of the corner of her eye, she saw it: a shadow that didn't belong.

There was no way it could have been just her reflection distorted in the puddles; it moved differently – too smooth, too fluid. It slithered along the wall like smoke, curling around the edges of the alley as if it had a mind of its own.

"W-what is it?" asked Harper, evidently perturbed by her sudden change in demeanour.

Chesney didn't answer. Her grip on the bat tightened, her pulse quickening as she watched the shadow shift. It wasn't her imagination. It was there, and it was wrong.

With a sharp breath, she forced herself to look away.

"Nothing," she muttered. "It's nothing."

Harper didn't look convinced, but he didn't push further. Chesney walked away, her boots clicking against the ground as she tried to shake the feeling of unseen eyes crawling across her skin.

Chapter Two

Chesney didn't head straight to The Pit. She never did. Walking into Delgado's den with her adrenaline still running high was a mistake she'd learned to avoid early on. Instead, she wound through the streets, letting the cold air clear her head.

The city had its own rhythm at night, a beat that never quite stopped. Cars rumbled in the distance, their tyres hissing over the wet pavement. Laughter spilled from the doorways of dive bars, mingling with the occasional scream or the unmistakable sound of a bottle smashing against the ground. This part of the city didn't sleep – it just changed faces when the sun went down.

Chesney slipped into another alley and leaned against the damp wall, letting her head fall back. Her fingers tapped absentmindedly against the bat, the metallic clink of her rings against the wood soothing her in a strange way.

That shadow in the alley: it hadn't been her imagination. She was sure of it. But what the hell could it have been?

She closed her eyes, replaying the scene in her mind. The way the shadow had moved, slithering across the brick like it was alive. It didn't make sense. Shadows didn't move like that, not unless something was casting them, but there hadn't been anything there to do that.

Her thoughts were interrupted by the clatter of an empty can rolling across the ground. Her eyes snapped open, her grip on her bat tightening as she scanned the alley.

"Relax, it's just me."

Chesney's shoulders dropped a fraction, and she exhaled through her nose.

"Jesus, Mikey," she said. "You're gonna get yourself killed, sneaking up on people like that."

Mikey stepped into the dim light, his hands raised in mock surrender. He was younger than Chesney by a couple of years, his wiry frame draped in a jacket two sizes too big. His mop of dark hair was perpetually messy, like he'd just rolled out of bed and hadn't bothered to check a mirror.

"Yeah, well, if it's you that kills me, at least it'll be quick," he said with a grin. "Delgado's got a different idea of "quick", if you know what I mean."

Chesney rolled her eyes.

"What do you want, Mikey?"

"Delgado's looking for you," he said. "Apparently, you were supposed to check-in an hour ago."

Chesney glanced at her watch and cursed under her breath. She hadn't realised how much time she'd spent wandering.

"Is he pissed off?"

"When isn't he?" Mikey said with a shrug. "Seriously though, no more than usual. You know how he is with his enforcers – just likes to keep tabs on people."

The way Mikey said it made Chesney's stomach turn. She hated that word. Enforcer. It made her sound like some hired thug who enjoyed busting heads for fun. That wasn't who she was, even if it was what she did.

"I'm on my way," she said, pushing off the wall.

Mikey fell into step beside her, his hands stuffed into his jacket pockets.

"Did you see anything weird tonight?" she asked him after a moment.

"Define "weird"," he said cynically, casting Chesney a sideways glance.

"Like... I don't know. Shadows moving when they shouldn't. That kind of thing."

"Can't say I have," Mikey said, frowning thoughtfully. "Why? Are you seeing ghosts now?"

Chesney didn't answer. She wasn't about to

tell him what she'd seen – or thought she'd seen. Mikey was alright, but he had a big mouth. The last thing she needed was for Delgado to hear about her "seeing things" and decide she wasn't reliable anymore.

"Forget it," she said.

Mikey shrugged again, but she could tell he wasn't convinced.

The Pit came into view as they rounded the corner, its neon sign buzzing faintly above the entrance. It wasn't much to look at – a squat: a brick building with barred windows and a door that looked like it had seen its fair share of battering rams. It was Delgado's base of operations.

Chesney took a deep breath and stepped inside, the familiar scent of stale beer and cigar smoke hitting her like a wall. The place was crowded, as usual, with Delgado's crew spread out across the mismatched furniture. Some played cards, others counted stacks of cash, and a few just sat around nursing drinks.

Delgado himself sat in the corner booth, his

hulking frame barely fitting into the space. His sharp suit was a stark contrast to the dingy surroundings, but the gold rings on his fingers and the ever-present cigar in his hand made him fit right in.

"Chesney," he called out, his voice booming over the noise. "You took your time."

She crossed the room, ignoring the stares from the other crew members. She could feel them looking at her, some curious, some hostile, but she didn't care. They knew better than to mess with her.

"Got held up," she said simply, sliding into the booth across from him.

"You got my money?" he asked, raising an eyebrow.

Chesney pulled a wad of cash from her pocket and dropped it on the table. It wasn't from Harper, it was hers, but she figured that Delgado didn't need to know that. She knew in her gut that Harper would pay up when she next saw him.

"Harper's good for the rest in three days," she said firmly.

Delgado picked up the money, thumbing through the bills with practiced ease.

"Three days, huh?" he muttered. "And you trust him to deliver?"

"I trust him to be too scared not to," she said.

Delgado chuckled, a low, rumbling sound that made Chesney's skin crawl.

"Fair enough," he said, still amused. "I've got another job for you."

Of course, thought Chesney. *There's always another job.*

"This one's a little more... delicate," he said, leaning forward. "Varga's crew has been stepping on my territory again. I want you to send a message."

Chesney frowned. Varga's crew was bad news. They played just as dirty as Delgado's guys – sometimes worse. Doing something to provoke them was like kicking a hornet's nest.

"What kind of message?" she asked.

"The kind they won't forget."

She resisted the urge to sigh. This wasn't what she'd signed up for when she started working for Delgado, but she didn't have much of a choice.

"Who will I be working with?"

Delgado grinned, and she immediately knew she wasn't going to like the answer.

"Noah," he said.

Chesney's stomach dropped. She stared at Delgado for a moment, waiting for him to laugh, to say it was a joke. But the smirk on his face told her he was serious. Dead serious.

"Noah?" she repeated, her voice flat.

Delgado's grin widened, showing too many teeth, all stained yellow with smoke.

"Is that a problem?" he asked firmly.

It was a problem. A big one. Noah was trouble, plain and simple. He'd only been with the crew for a few months, but he'd already gained a reputation for being reckless. He was the kind of guy who liked to make a scene, who didn't know the meaning of the word "subtle". As someone who prided herself on her ability to get in and out of a situation without drawing unnecessary attention, Chesney knew that having to work with Noah would be a recipe for disaster.

"I work better alone," she said, keeping her tone even.

"Not this time," Delgado said, leaning back in the booth. "This job's too big for one person. You're gonna need backup."

Chesney clenched her jaw, biting back the string of curses that threatened to spill out. Delgado wasn't going to budge, and arguing with him would only make her look weak.

"Fine," she said tightly. "When do we start?"

"Tomorrow night," Delgado said, puffing on his cigar. "I'll have the details sent to you in the morning."

Chesney nodded her head, her movements stiff as she stood.

"Don't screw this up, Chesney," Delgado called after her as she headed for the door.

She didn't bother responding.

The cold air hit her like a slap in the face as she stepped out of The Pit.

"Looks like someone's not happy," Mikey said, falling into step beside her.

"Damn right," Chesney snapped, her patience already worn thin. "I've got to work with Noah."

"Hey, no need to bite my head off," Mikey said, holding up his hands. "Noah's not so bad once you get to know him."

Chesney shot Mikey a glare.

"I don't need to "get to know him"," she said. "I need him to do his job and stay out of my way."

Mikey raised an eyebrow, but didn't say anything else. They walked in silence for a while, the sound of their footsteps echoing off the buildings around them. Chesney's mind was racing, trying to piece together how she was going to handle this.

Noah. Of all the people Delgado could've picked, it had to be him. She'd worked hard to build her reputation, to prove she wasn't just another thug. And now she was being saddled with the one guy who seemed determined to embody every stereotype about their line of work.

"Maybe it won't be so bad," Mikey said after a while, his tone almost hopeful.

"Yeah," Chesney scoffed doubtfully, "and maybe pigs will fly."

***

Chesney didn't go straight home. She couldn't – not like this, not with her head spinning. Her girlfriend already worried about her enough, always bracing for the worst call or a knock on the door. Going back to their flat worked up and frantic would only make it worse. Chesney couldn't bear the thought of adding to that burden.

Instead, she made her way to the rooftop of

an abandoned building a few blocks away, one of her favourite places to clear her head. The city stretched out below her, a maze of lights and shadows. This was her world, for better or worse. She didn't know how to live any differently.

She sat on the edge of the roof, her legs dangling over the side, and stared out at the skyline. The shadow she'd seen earlier was still nagging at her, a question she couldn't shake.

It wasn't just the way it had moved – it was the way it had felt. Like it was watching her. Like it knew her.

She shook her head, trying to dispel the thought. She was just tired, perhaps, and maybe the stress of working for Delgado was finally getting to her.

Chapter Three

The door to the apartment clicked softly as Chesney stepped inside, her boots squeaking against the hardwood floor. She pulled off her hoodie and hung it on the peg by the door, relieved to have its weight no longer on her. The familiar scent of lavender and chamomile hung in the air, mingling with the faint aroma of freshly brewed tea that always seemed to linger in their home. Jade loved tea.

The apartment was small but warm, a stark contrast to the sprawling city outside. The walls were painted in shades of cream and pale green, decorated with framed prints of blooming flowers and poetry excerpts in looping, elegant script. The living area was dominated by a second-hand couch piled high with mismatched cushions and a knitted throw that Jade had made last winter.

A tiny kitchenette was tucked into one corner, its countertops cluttered with jars of herbs and spices, a drying rack of mugs, and a small vase of flowers Jade had purchased from one of the local boutiques. A bookshelf by the window overflowed with novels and notepads, its bottom shelf crowded with Chesney's collection of old vinyls and a battered record player.

Chesney leaned against the edge of the couch, letting out a long breath. The subtle ticking of the clock on the wall drew her gaze. 3:07am. She cursed under her breath. It was too late – or too early – for anyone to be awake, but then again, Jade rarely kept normal hours. The thought of her girlfriend made Chesney's heart ache with equal parts longing and guilt. Jade didn't deserve this. The worry. The uncertainty. The countless nights spent wondering if Chesney would come home in one piece.

"Chesney?"

Chesney jumped, her heart skipping a beat. She turned to see Jade standing in the doorway of the bedroom, her figure framed by the glow of a bedside lamp. Her long black hair was tied back in a neat bun, strands escaping to frame her heart-shaped face. She wore one of Chesney's oversized hoodies over a pair of pale pink pyjama bottoms, the sleeves pushed up to reveal her slender wrists.

"Sorry, I didn't mean to wake you," Chesney said.

"You didn't," said Jade, her voice reassuring as she stepped into the room. "I was up writing... Are you hungry? I can make you some tea and a sandwich."

Chesney blinked, the offer catching her off guard.

"Jade, it's just past three in the morning."

"So?" Jade said with a smile, already moving towards the kitchenette. "You've had a long night. I don't mind."

As she watched Jade, Chesney felt the tension in her body loosen, just a little. To be in Jade's presence was like stepping into a safe harbour after battling a storm. Chesney often told herself she didn't deserve Jade – not her kindness, not her patience, not the quiet stability she brought to their chaotic life. And yet, here was Jade standing in their shared kitchen a little after three in the morning, ready to make her a cup of tea.

Jade moved gracefully, pulling out a loaf of bread and a block of cheese. Chesney continued to watch, unable to suppress a small smile. They were opposites in almost every way. Where Chesney was brash and rough around the edges, Jade was gentle and polished. Even their appearances reflected the contrast: Chesney with her long blonde hair streaked with pink, her punky clothes, her dark hoodies and leather jackets; Jade with her neat bun, soft sweaters, and floral skirts. And yet, somehow, they worked so well together.

Jade glanced over her shoulder, her expression tender with concern.

"You seem stressed," she said. "Do you want to talk about it?"

Chesney shook her head quickly.

"It's nothing," she insisted. "Just a long night."

Jade didn't press, but her gaze lingered. She set a steaming mug of tea on the low table in the living area, then handed Chesney a plate with a grilled cheese sandwich, the crust golden and the cheese perfectly melted. Chesney accepted it with a murmured "thanks" and sat down on the couch.

"You're wonderful, you know that?" Jade said softly, sitting across from her. "You could do anything, Chesney. Anything. You don't have to keep doing this... dangerous work."

The words hit Chesney like a blow, her throat tightening. She looked down at her sandwich, her appetite suddenly gone. She wanted to believe Jade, to let those words wrap around her like a blanket and banish the doubts that gnawed at her. But she couldn't. Not entirely. Anxiety and depression had been her constant companions for years, and the thought of a "normal" job felt impossibly out of reach. She'd tried before and failed. Working for Delgado wasn't what she wanted, wasn't what she would have preferred, but it paid well, and she'd fallen into it because it was easier than trying and failing again.

"You're sweet," she said, her voice tight, "but I'm not cut out for much else."

"That's not true," Jade said firmly, reaching out and taking Chesney's hand, her grasp warm and steady. "You're capable of so much more than you think. And no matter what, I'm here for you. I'll always support you."

Chesney felt tears prickling at the corners of her eyes, but blinked them away, swallowing hard. Sometimes it hurt when Jade was so nice to her.

"Thanks, Jade," she said.

"Why don't you let me run you a bath?" Jade suggested, squeezing her hand. "It'll help you relax."

Chesney hesitated, then nodded.

"That sounds nice," she said, genuinely appreciative of the kind offer.

"Finish your tea," Jade said, standing and brushing her hands against her pyjama bottoms. "I'll go and light some candles."

Chesney watched her go, overwhelmed with gratitude and guilt. She drank her tea in silence, the warmth of it soothing, but not enough to vanquish the storm in her mind.

The bath was steaming and fragrant with lavender oil. Chesney slid into the water, letting out a long sigh as the heat seeped into her muscles. She leaned back, her head resting against the rim of the tub, and closed her eyes. The events of the night replayed in her mind, from Harper's panicked excuses, to the shadow that had moved wrong, to Delgado's smirk when he'd assigned her to work with Noah. It all felt like too much.

When the water began to cool, Chesney got out. She grabbed a towel and dried herself as she padded into the bedroom. Jade was already under the duvet, her side lamp still on. She held it open for Chesney, who climbed in beside her. Without a word, Jade put an arm around her, pulling her close. Her embrace was a balm to Chesney's frayed nerves.

"Goodnight," Jade murmured sleepily.

"Goodnight," Chesney whispered.

Jade's breathing soon evened out, her arm still draped over Chesney. But Chesney lay awake, staring ahead, her thoughts circling like vultures. She felt safe here with Jade, but it didn't erase the worries clawing at her mind. She closed her eyes, willing herself to sleep, but it didn't come easily.

Chapter Four

Chesney awoke alone, the duvet tangled around her limbs as if she had been struggling in her sleep. She took a moment to collect herself, her eyes adjusting to the dim light that filtered in through the curtains. She figured that Jade had gone out to meet a writing client and had been quiet so as not to wake her.

With a sigh, Chesney rolled over and reached for her phone on the nightstand. She was greeted by the insistent buzz of a message. She groaned at the thought of having to deal with anything before she had even had her coffee.

As she squinted at the screen, irritated by its bright glow, she instantly recognised the sender. Delgado. Her stomach sank. She debated whether to open the message now or wait until she was better equipped to handle whatever it may contain, but her curiosity got the better of her.

Meeting point at the docks. Port A12. 10pm.

She let her arm drop, the phone landing on the mattress with a muted thud. She rubbed her hand over her face, as if she could wipe away the growing sense of dread that accompanied every interaction connected to Delgado.

As she inhaled slowly to calm her nerves, Chesney caught the faint scent of lavender – Jade's hand cream. A welcome distraction. For a moment, she let herself lie there, staring up at the ceiling. She knew, however, that no matter how she played it, time was ticking and she couldn't get out of tonight's meeting, no matter how much she wanted to.

Chesney finally swung her legs over the side of the bed. She sat there for a moment, rubbing the sleep from her eyes and trying to shake off the heavy fog of restlessness that clung to her. She then pushed herself up and padded towards the kitchenette, her steps slow and uneven as though she was carrying her worries with her.

The faint aroma of brewed coffee lingered in the air. Jade's touch was everywhere – the tidy counters, the neatly stacked mugs, the fresh vase of daisies sitting by the window. Chesney's gaze fell to the counter where a folded note sat propped against the sugar jar.

Meeting a client – might be back late. There's coffee on the stove. Love you. – J.

Chesney smiled faintly, her fingers brushing over the handwriting. Jade always thought of the little things, the details that made life a little easier.

The day stretched along, empty and restless. Chesney spent most of it pacing the apartment, the stillness unnerving in a way she couldn't articulate. Every creak of the floorboards, every tick of the clock, seemed louder than usual. She went over the possible scenarios again and again, playing out how the meeting with Noah might go. Delgado's text hadn't offered much detail, but she knew better than to expect anything simple.

She thought to herself about how Jade was probably sitting in some cosy café in a nice part of the city, meeting with a ghostwriting client, likely someone paying her to pen another one of those sweet, idyllic small-town romances she had a knack for. It suited Jade perfectly – her soft voice, her gentle laugh, her ability to tease out emotions and package them into something warm and beautiful.

Chesney, meanwhile, had a meeting at the docks with a thug who thought smoking and swearing was a personality.

Noah. Even his name was enough to set her teeth on edge. She didn't trust him – not his attitude, not his impulsiveness, not his overconfidence. If things went sideways tonight, it wouldn't be him picking up the pieces.

When it was time, as the familiar itch of anxiety clawed at her, Chesney grabbed her jacket, checked the weight of the bat in her hand, and left.

***

The docks were a patchwork of shadows and light, the glow of streetlamps reflecting off the water in jagged shards. The air smelt of salt and diesel, and the distant sound of subtle waves was the only noise breaking the silence.

Chesney scanned the area, her sharp eyes landing on a figure leaning against a shipping container.

Noah.

The orange glow of his cigarette lit up his face, highlighting the smirk she hated.

"Hey there, partner," he drawled, flicking the cigarette away as she approached. "Ready to raise some hell?"

Chesney ignored him, shoving her hands into her jacket pockets as she walked past, expecting him to follow her to avoid loitering and drawing attention.

"Not much of a talker, huh?" Noah said, pushing off the container and falling into step beside her. "That's cool. I can do the talking for both of us. Relax, sweetheart. I've got your back."

Chesney tightened her jaw in irritation. She

stopped abruptly, turning on him so fast he almost stumbled.

"First of all, don't call me sweetheart," she said, her tone like ice. "Second, if you screw this up, I'll make sure you regret it. Got it?"

He raised his hands in mock surrender, the smirk never leaving his face.

"Ok, ok," he said. "Chill the fuck out."

Chesney didn't respond. Her grip on her bat tightened, her knuckles whitening. She had a bad feeling about this.

As she continued to walk, looking for port A12, Noah trailed behind her, his boots crunching against the gravel. He was humming a tune under his breath, something low and off-key that made her teeth clench.

"Could you not?" she snapped quietly, venom lacing her words as she shot him a glare over her shoulder.

"Could I not what?" he asked innocently, his annoying grin widening.

"Humming. Breathing. Existing. Take your pick."

"Wow, you're a ray of sunshine, aren't you?"

Chesney didn't respond. She didn't have the patience for Noah's antics, not when her nerves were already stretched thin. Delgado's jobs were never straightforward, and this one was shaping up to be no exception.

They reached the meeting point: a cluster of rusted shipping containers stacked high, their sides streaked with grime and graffiti. Chesney scanned the area, taking in every detail – the shadows between the containers, the faint hum of a generator somewhere in the distance, the creak of metal shifting in the breeze.

Noah leaned casually against one of the containers, crossing his arms.

"So, what are we waiting for?" he asked, his tone light.

"Delgado's contact," Chesney muttered pointedly, hoping Noah would take the hint and lower his voice.

As if on cue, a figure stepped out from the shadows, tall and broad-shouldered with a face that looked like it had been carved from stone. He was dressed in a black trench coat, the collar pulled up against the wind.

"Chesney?" the man asked, his voice deep and gravelly.

"Who's asking?" she said bluntly.

The man didn't answer. Instead, he reached into his coat and pulled out a black duffel bag, tossing it at her feet.

"Everything you need is in there," he said. "Blueprints, codes, and a burner phone. You've got one shot at this, so don't screw it up."

Chesney crouched down, unzipping the bag just enough to peek inside. Sure enough, there was a stack of papers, a small black device, and a handful of tools she didn't recognise.

"What's the target?" she asked, standing.

"Varga's hideout," the man said plainly, his

expression unchanging. "The boss wants to get a message to them, loud and clear. Details are in the bag."

Chesney's stomach tightened. She was practically being asked to feed herself to the lions. Varga's crew wasn't just another gang. They were ruthless, unpredictable, known for turning even minor disputes into bloodbaths. If Delgado wanted to send a message, it wouldn't just be loud – it would provoke a roar in return.

Her mind churned through every possibility, every outcome. If things went south, Noah wasn't the kind of backup she could count on. Would Delgado send someone else to pull her out if she was trapped? No. She was expendable to him, just another throwaway tool in his arsenal.

The stakes were clear, but what if the price of success was her life?

Chapter Five

Before Chesney could press further, the man turned and walked away, disappearing back into the shadows as quickly as he'd appeared.

"Well, he seems fun," Noah said, kicking at the gravel.

Chesney ignored him, slinging the duffel bag over her shoulder.

"Let's go," she said, already confident that Noah had brought his car. "Somewhere quiet and out of the way. We need to get to grips with what's in the bag, and how we're gonna approach this."

Chesney assessed Noah's car with thinly veiled disdain as she approached. It was an old, battered saloon with a dented bumper and peeling paint, its age betrayed by the dull sheen of rust creeping along the edges. She opened the passenger door, wincing as it let out a groan of protest, and slid inside, the seat cushion sagging under her weight.

The interior wasn't much better. Fast food wrappers littered the floor, and a faint but pervasive stench of cigarettes clung to everything – from the stained fabric seats to the scratched plastic dashboard. A crumpled energy drink can rolled under her feet as she adjusted herself, grimacing.

The radio was an ancient, dented relic, its buttons mismatched and worn smooth. Chesney had barely fastened her seatbelt when Noah turned the key in the ignition, causing the engine to cough to life with a sputtering rumble.

Instantly, the car was filled with ear-splitting techno music, the bass pounding so hard it made Chesney's teeth rattle. She shot Noah a sharp look, her annoyance cutting through the din.

He smirked, one hand on the wheel as he reached out with the other to jab the radio's power button, cutting off the music mid-beat.

"Not a fan of tunes?" he asked, the faintest hint of mockery in his tone.

"Not that kind," she replied bluntly.

Noah chuckled to himself and shifted the car into gear, pulling away from the curb with a jerk. They merged into the flow of the city's nighttime traffic, the glow of streetlights and neon signs casting fractured reflections on the windshield.

"Head to the abandoned adult cinema," Chesney instructed. "We'll use the green room in there. There's no point going to The Pit; it will be too loud and I don't fancy going over this with Delgado looking over our shoulders."

"Cool, ok," said Noah, a playful smirk crossing his features.

Grow up, Chesney thought.

The rest of the drive was tense, the silence broken only by the occasional scrape of

Noah's lighter as he flicked it open and closed. Chesney looked out of the window, her thoughts racing, her fingers drumming against the bat on her knees as she scanned the passing buildings.

Something about this job didn't sit right with her. The man at the docks had been too vague, too evasive.

"You're very quiet," Noah said, his voice cutting through the silence.

"I'm thinking," Chesney said shortly.

"About what?"

"About how this job is probably going to get us killed."

"Relax," said Noah, calmly keeping his eyes on the road ahead. "It's just a job like any other."

Chesney didn't respond. She knew better than to believe it would be that simple. It was alarmingly clear to her that Noah was blissfully unaware of the dangers of this particular job. As soon as Delgado had mentioned a personal rival, Chesney had known this job would have "trouble" written all over it.

Noah eased the car into a spot a few blocks away from their destination, pulling it close to the curb with a practiced nonchalance. He cut the engine, and the car gave a reluctant sputter before falling silent. The street was dimly lit, the glow from a nearby flickering streetlamp casting long, jagged shadows over the pavement. As they stepped out of the vehicle, Chesney was hit by the unpleasant smell in the air, a faint metallic lustre that made her wince.

The walk to the abandoned cinema took them through a neighbourhood caught in a perpetual state of decay. Boarded-up windows stared blankly out from weathered buildings, all covered in graffiti sprawled across the brick walls.

Looming ahead, the cinema itself was a hulking relic of a bygone era, its façade a patchwork of peeling paint and cracked plaster. The doors, which had once been ornate glass, were now shattered and boarded up with sheets of warped plywood.

Weeds grew in uneven clumps along the edges of the building, their roots pushing through the pavement.

Chesney and Noah entered the building through a discreet side door. The air was stale, and as they navigated past shattered furniture and decaying props, remnants of the cinema's scandalous history were impossible to ignore. Among the debris, discarded tools of taboo pleasures – sex toys and BDSM gear – were strewn about in disarray.

Chesney confidently pushed open the green room door, a space she was well-acquainted with from past endeavours, but only in her capacity as an enforcer working for Delgado. Noah trailed in after her, plopping down on a worn leather sofa with a smirk playing on his lips. His gaze swept over the room, taking in the sight of chains, whips, and aged magazines scattered sporadically around them.

"Right," said Chesney, hoping that Noah would start to grasp the seriousness of the job, "let's get on with it."

She delved into the bag and spread the blueprints out on the low table, studying them with a critical eye. The building they were expected to infiltrate was a fortress – with motion sensors, security cameras, and guards patrolling every floor.

"Fucking hell," said Noah, leaning forward. "This place is guarded more tightly than a bank."

"Exactly," said Chesney, still in shock that Delgado was expecting them to go there.

She delved into the bag again, and retrieved a single folded bit of paper and a small black device. Her breath caught as she carefully unfolded the paper, revealing a crudely drawn map and a single word: "Plant". Her eyes widened as she recognised the device for what it was: an explosive to be planted in enemy territory.

Noah's expression darkened as the enormity of the situation began to dawn on him, his usual cockiness melting away. Chesney's hand trembled slightly as she held the device. She bit down on her lower lip, her instincts screaming at her to walk away. But Delgado's jobs weren't optional; she was terrified by even the thought of telling him she wanted out.

Chapter Six

Chesney sat on the worn-out sofa of the green room, her bat resting against her knee, its wood glinting faintly in the dim light of the single working bulb above. Across from her, Noah sprawled with his typical lazy confidence, a notebook balanced on one knee, a pen twirling absently in his fingers.

They had been trying to figure this out over several nights now. Each time, they had picked up where they'd left off, brainstorming plans and running through potential scenarios, yet the map spread out on the battered coffee table between them remained as much a mystery as when they'd first started.

"This is hopeless," said Noah, letting out a sigh as he tossed his pen onto the table in frustration. "There's no way we can get in without being seen."

Chesney leaned back into the sofa, pinching the bridge of her nose.

"There must be something that we're missing here," she muttered. "There has to be a way. Delgado wouldn't have given an impossible job."

"True," said Noah, "but he won't care if we don't make it out alive. Even if we break into Varga's place and get killed on the spot, Delgado will still have the satisfaction of knowing that he's at least done something to fuck with his rival."

Chesney shot Noah a dark look. She hadn't thought of it like that before, and she hated the fact that he was probably right.

"That's not helpful," she finally said, blunt and frustrated.

For a moment, the only sound was the occasional groan of the building settling, as if the old cinema itself was tired of their presence. Chesney let out a heavy sigh, then stood, her grip firm on her bat.

"I need to clear my head," she said. "I'm going out for some air. I'll be back soon enough."

Noah looked up, his usual smugness giving way to something resembling concern.

"Are you ok?" he asked.

"I will be," she said, already making her way towards the exit.

The night air outside was cool and damp, the pavement slick from a recent spell of rain. Chesney walked briskly away from the cinema, her bat a comforting weight in her hand. She focused on the rhythm of her footsteps and the steady inhale-exhale of her breath, trying to ground herself.

Her chest felt tight, and her pulse was erratic. She recognised the signs creeping up on her: she could feel a panic attack brewing just beneath the surface.

Not now. Please not now, she thought.

Spotting the mouth of an alley, she ducked

into the shadows and leaned against the brick wall. The familiar rituals began: counting her breaths, grounding herself by naming the textures around her – the roughness of the wall at her back, the grit of the pavement under her boots, the damp chill of the air against her skin.

She didn't know how long she'd been standing there, but eventually, the pressure in her chest began to ease, the frantic beat of her heart slowing to something more manageable.

Then she saw it.

A shadow detached itself from the wall across from her, a ripple of darkness that moved with an unsettling, fluid grace. It wasn't tethered to anything solid, no light source casting it in any direction. Chesney's breath caught in her throat, her fingers once again tightening around the bat.

The shadow hovered for a moment, amorphous but vaguely humanoid in shape, then shifted, as if tilting its head towards her.

"Who's there?" Chesney demanded, her voice

trembling despite her attempt to sound firm.

The shadow didn't answer, but its presence seemed to change. The air, which had felt oppressive just moments before, grew lighter, almost comforting.

And then the voice came. Soft, distorted, undeniably female, it echoed in Chesney's mind rather than her ears:

"Do not trust Delgado. Do not go through with this job."

The words sent a jolt through Chesney. She swallowed hard, her mind racing.

"I don't have a choice," she murmured aloud. "You don't just walk away from Delgado."

There was no response, no shift in the air to suggest the shadow had even heard her. It had gone, just as suddenly as it had appeared, leaving Chesney standing alone in the alley.

Realising that she must have raised her bat defensively when the shadow had first made its presence known, Chesney's hands shook as she lowered the weapon. Whatever that thing was, it was unlike anything she had ever had to deal with before.

Barely able to think straight anymore, she grabbed her phone from her pocket. She immediately began tapping the screen to send a text to Noah:

I'm feeling unwell. Heading home. You should do the same. Take everything with you.

Sliding the phone back into her pocket, she exhaled a shaky breath and headed out of the alley. She hoped Noah wouldn't question her sudden departure. If he did, she'd find a way to deflect it tomorrow. Right now, she just needed to get away – to the quiet of her apartment, to the safety of its walls, to the comfort of Jade's gentle presence.

Chapter Seven

The city at night was a strange mix of stillness and chaos. Chesney's boots echoed against the concrete as she walked, the rhythmic steps matching the restless beat of her thoughts. She'd told Noah she was going home, and she'd meant it – every cell in her body screamed for rest. But as she passed a flickering streetlamp, her mind jolted her with an icy realisation: she'd forgotten about Harper.

Delgado would be expecting the money. No excuses, no delays.

"Damn it," she muttered irritably, rubbing her temples.

How had she let this slip? It wasn't just an oversight; it was a mistake that could cost her dearly. Her chest tightened as she pictured

Delgado's stern face, imagining the fury that would erupt if she didn't deliver.

Her body sagged with weariness, but her mind snapped into focus. She didn't have a choice – home would have to wait. With a resigned sigh, she tightened her grip on her bat and turned towards the opposite end of the city.

The walk felt endless. The streets grew quieter the further she went, the hum of traffic thinning until the only sounds were the rustling of litter in the wind and the distant bark of a stray dog. Each step felt heavier than the last, but she pushed forward, fuelled by equal parts fear and determination.

By the time she reached the familiar alley where she expected Harper to be waiting, her nerves were frayed. The fluorescent lights from nearby cast eerie shadows, and for a moment, she hesitated. But then she saw him, lounging against a brick wall, hands in his pockets, looking as awkward as ever.

Chesney squared her shoulders and adopted the mask she knew too well: cold, unyielding, dangerous.

"Harper," she called quietly as she neared him, her voice cutting through the night like a blade.

His head snapped up, and she saw the flash of recognition – and fear – in his eyes. Good.

"Ch-Chesney," he stuttered, attempting a smile. "I was just..."

"Save it," she said, taking a step closer to him, her bat resting casually against her shoulder. "Have you got my money, or am I going to have to remind you why this isn't a negotiation?"

"I've got it, I've got it," he rambled. "No need for any of that; I don't want any trouble."

From his jacket, he pulled out a thick wad of cash, holding it out with shaking hands. Chesney took it, flipping through it quickly to ensure the amount was right.

"Smart move," she said coolly, stuffing the bills into her pocket.

A brief spark of relief coursed through her; at least that was one problem down, even if it wasn't the main one.

Turning on her heel, she walked briskly away, her fingers brushing the edge of the cash. She'd skim a bit for herself to make up for what she had given Delgado the other night.

The Pit was buzzing when Chesney arrived, the low hum of conversation and occasional bursts of laughter filling the smoky air. Delgado sat at the head of the room, his bulky frame dominating the space. A cigar rested between his fingers, the acrid smoke curling lazily around him as his entourage hung on his every word.

Chesney approached, weaving through the crowd until she stood before him. Delgado's dark eyes flicked to her, and he smiled, the kind of grin that made her stomach churn.

"I trust you got Harper to pay up?" he asked, his voice smooth but with an edge that warned against disappointment. "I've been waiting."

"It's done," said Chesney, careful to keep her expression neutral as she handed over the cash.

Delgado thumbed through the bills, nodding in satisfaction.

"Good," he said. "I trust everything's going well with your new assignment?"

"Yes," said Chesney, forcing herself to nod. "All under control."

Delgado raised an eyebrow, his gaze piercing. He didn't say anything, but the look he gave her – a silent warning – spoke volumes. Chesney swallowed hard, hoping he couldn't see the cracks in her façade.

Satisfied, Delgado turned away, engaging someone else in his entourage. Chesney took a step back, ready to make her exit, when the voice struck again:

"You can't trust him."

Chesney froze, her blood turning to ice. It was the same voice – that eerie, feminine tone – she'd heard in the alley.

"Look at him," the voice urged. *"See him for what he truly is: a demon in human form."*

Chesney's breath hitched, panic clawing at her chest. She glanced at Delgado, but he seemed the same as always: boisterous, commanding, human.

"He's not what he appears to be," the voice pressed. *"You would do well to sever all ties with him."*

Chesney's grip on her bat tightened as she fought to keep her composure. She couldn't let anyone see her fear, couldn't let them know she was unravelling. She forced her feet to move, retreating step by step until she slipped out of The Pit and into the cool night.

Outside, she gulped for air, the city's chaos dulling the pounding in her head. She needed to get home. Whatever was happening – whether it was stress, paranoia, or something else entirely – she couldn't deal with it here.

Chapter Eight

The city streets transformed into a sprawling, ever-shifting landscape of greys and blacks. Shadows danced around Chesney as she made her way through the predawn silence, her breathing uneven and laboured. Her fingers, still tightly gripping her bat, now trembled with fear and adrenaline as she tried to suppress the panic rising within her. In her current state, after everything that had happened tonight, it was a constant battle between mind and body.

Come on, Chesney, don't give in to it, she told herself with fierce determination. She hated the thought of letting her guard down in this moment of vulnerability.

The strange, otherworldly whisper that had slithered through her mind still echoed in her thoughts, a haunting reminder: Do not trust Delgado. But how could she possibly free herself from Delgado's intricate, potentially lethal web? The extent of his influence seemed to stretch far beyond her immediate comprehension, weaving through the complex network of the city's entire underworld.

Chesney's every step in the direction of home became a deliberate, almost ritualistic act of pure willpower. Breathe in. Count methodically. Breathe out. Maintain control. The therapeutic techniques a counsellor had meticulously taught her years earlier resurfaced with the precision of muscle memory, a survival mechanism hardwired into her. Her chest felt constricted, her lungs struggling against an invisible compression that threatened to suffocate her from within.

I mustn't have a panic attack, she told herself. *Not now in the streets, and not when I get home. Not in front of Jade – she might still be awake. I need to stay composed.*

As Chesney neared her apartment building, instead of the sight offering comfort, it triggered a fresh, overwhelming wave of anxiety that threatened to destabilise her.

How could she possibly articulate the night's surreal and terrifying events to Jade: the shadow, the disembodied voice, Varga's seemingly impenetrable fortress, and Delgado's increasingly dangerous commands?

The simple answer was clear: she couldn't. She wouldn't.

Despite her fragile state, Chesney diligently turned her key in the lock. She stepped inside their apartment with calculated movements, setting her bat down with exquisite, almost choreographed care. Each motion was designed to produce minimal sound, a survival instinct honed through previous dangerous encounters on the streets. She looked at the clock and exhaled slowly, slightly relieved. It was 4:55am. Jade would be asleep, she assumed.

Chesney plopped down onto the couch and sat there quietly for a moment, almost believing she could hold herself together. But then she cracked. Sobs erupted from the deepest recesses of her chest – raw, uncontrollable sounds that seemed to tear themselves violently from her very core.

These were not merely tears, but a profound, visceral release of accumulated trauma, fear, and unprocessed emotion.

Curled up vulnerably with her head in her hands, Chesney felt Jade before she saw her; the precise pressure of her embrace, the distinctive lavender scent, the soft, rhythmic murmur of comfort were all instantly recognisable.

"I'm here," Jade whispered, gentle but firm. "I'm right here."

Chesney's sobs gradually subsided into exhausted, hiccupping sniffles. She felt hollowed out, drained of everything except a profound, aching gratitude that settled around her like a protective blanket. She was acutely aware of her physical vulnerability – the trembling hands, the raw throat, the total emotional exhaustion that made even simple movements feel monumental.

"Stay here," said Jade, her voice a careful blend of command and comfort. "I'll get you something warm."

Chesney watched through blurry, swollen

eyes as Jade busily prepared something in the compact kitchenette with characteristic grace, fluid and deliberate. Her mind continued to churn, replaying the night's events with a merciless, cinematographic precision.

Fortunately, it wasn't long before Chesney was presented with a steaming mug of tea, accompanied by a plate of lightly buttered toast. These simple, caring offerings from Jade felt like pure salvation, a lifeline pulling her back from the edge.

Jade settled beside Chesney on the couch, positioning herself with tact – close enough to offer comfort, but not so intrusive as to be overbearing. Her worry was palpable, etched into the slight furrow of her brow and the careful way her eyes tracked Chesney's every movement and expression.

"Do you want to talk?" Jade asked patiently after several minutes of weighted silence, her voice an invitation rather than a demand.

Chesney's throat tightened, a physical manifestation of the emotional barriers she was desperately trying to maintain. Talk about what, exactly? The strange warning from a voice that defied all rational explanation? The potentially suicidal job for Delgado? The constant, gnawing fear that saturated her existence – the terrifying possibility that one day, she might not make it home?

"Not right now," she managed, the words emerging as a ragged whisper.

"Ok," said Jade, understanding flooding through her expression. "Whatever it is you need, I'm here."

The promise of sanctuary, of unconditional support, made Chesney's eyes well up again.

"I'll run a bath for you, make more tea, hold you close," Jade whispered, her voice soothing.

In that moment, Chesney loved her with a ferocity that transcended conventional wisdom – a love that was part survival instinct, part pure emotional connection, part desperate hope.

As the first tentative rays of dawn began to

infiltrate the apartment's carefully drawn curtains, pale light transformed the space. Chesney's breathing slowly synchronised with Jade's, a rhythmic counterpoint to the city's awakening sounds. Beneath the momentary peace, however, Chesney's mind continued to simmer. The shadow in the alley. The voice that had weaved its way through her head. The warning about Delgado. The job with Noah that looked close to impossible. None of them had been resolved – just temporarily suspended. They waited, like predators just beyond the periphery of time, patient and inevitable.

She closed her eyes, allowing Jade's steady presence to anchor her in this fragile moment of reprieve. But she knew, with a gut-churning certainty, that the same problems would be there tomorrow.

Chapter Nine

Chesney's eyes flickered open with a languid, almost reluctant movement. The light filtering in through the bedroom's neatly drawn curtains had a soft, diffused quality that seemed to blur the boundaries between sleep and wakefulness. Her head felt impossibly heavy, weighed down by the remnants of exhaustion and fragmented dreams.

She rolled over with a groan, her hand outstretched and fumbling across the bed for her phone. When she finally grabbed it and blinked at the screen, the time read 12:17pm. Relief swept through her as she saw no messages or missed calls, her phone's inactivity a small mercy. It didn't surprise her that she had woken up so late – the previous night's torment had drained her, and she still didn't feel one-hundred percent right.

The familiar, comforting scent of freshly brewed coffee preceded Jade's arrival into the room. She appeared in the doorway like a vision of domestic grace, a steaming ceramic mug cradled in her hands. Her dark hair was pulled back in a loose ponytail that highlighted the elegant line of her jaw, and she was wearing pastel-pink pyjama trousers with one of Chesney's oversized hoodies.

"Morning, beautiful," Jade said, her voice modulated to a pitch that suggested both concern and tenderness.

She approached the bed carefully, as though navigating a delicate emotional landscape.

Chesney managed a smile, grateful but tired as she pushed herself up against the headboard with movements that spoke of profound physical exhaustion. The mug Jade offered was warm between her hands, its heat seeping into her palms, providing a grounding sensation that helped anchor her to the present moment.

"You're an angel," Chesney mumbled, the words emerging raggedly as she brushed a pink strand of hair from her face.

"I'm staying home today," Jade announced as she perched herself on the edge of the bed. "I need to know that you're ok."

Something profound and complex stirred within Chesney – a turbulent mixture of gratitude, guilt, and a deep, almost overwhelming sense of being truly seen and cared for.

"You don't have to do that," she protested weakly, the words a reflexive response more than genuine resistance.

"I want to," said Jade. "I'm hoping you'll take the night off. Just rest. Recuperate."

"I can't," Chesney said, wishing that she could. "There's a job. A big one."

Jade's eyes, deep and perceptive, seemed to hold an empathy that went beyond ordinary understanding. They weren't just focused on Chesney's face; they were searching, as if trying to unravel the intricate emotions hidden beneath her expression.

"Is that why you were so upset last night?"

Chesney hesitated. There was no way she could even begin to explain. She couldn't bear the thought of burdening Jade with everything she was up against.

"Partly," she finally managed.

Jade's kindness was almost unbearable – a pure, unfiltered compassion that made Chesney feel so guilty.

"It's ok," said Jade. "I won't pry. Just know that I'll listen if you change your mind."

Jade's gaze lingered on Chesney, her brows knitting ever so slightly in that way they did when she was piecing things together. Chesney felt exposed under that look.

"I just want you to know that whatever it is that's bothering you at the moment," Jade said, her voice careful as if trying not to spook Chesney, "I can see that it must be a big deal. Please, please remember that you're wonderful, Chesney. You can do anything you set your mind to. You deserve so much more than this job that seems to come with so much fear, so much danger. I know you don't like to tell me the details of what you're up against, but it pains me to think that you're going through something that is clearly upsetting you so much."

Unable to articulate the messy web of circumstances that kept her tethered to Delgado's world – the complex network of obligations, threats, and intricate personal compromises – Chesney simply whispered a request that was simultaneously a plea and a surrender:

"Hold me?"

Jade nodded without hesitation, her expression softening into something wholly understanding. She shifted her weight, moving fluidly from the edge of the bed to join Chesney under the duvet. Jade settled beside Chesney and gently wrapped her arm around her shoulders, drawing her close.

Chesney leaned into the embrace, resting her head against Jade's collarbone, the faint scent of lavender grounding her in the moment.

Jade's hand found Chesney's, her fingers intertwining in a silent reassurance.

"I've got you," Jade murmured, her voice low and steady.

Chesney exhaled shakily, allowing herself to relax into the warmth and safety of Jade's hold.

***

The day with Jade had been nothing short of lovely. They'd spent the afternoon in quiet companionship – sharing light conversation, indulging in Jade's homemade cakes, and even binge-watching one of Jade's favourite cosy dramas. For a few hours, Chesney had managed to push the darkness of her world to the periphery, allowing herself to be anchored by Jade's warmth and laughter.

But still the fear of the night had loomed like a storm cloud on the horizon, casting a shadow over every moment. No matter how hard Chesney had tried to immerse herself in the simplicity of their day, the thought of the job, and of everything that came with venturing out into the city's dangerous underbelly, lingered constantly at the edges of her mind.

As twilight gave way to night, Chesney's steps felt heavier with each block she crossed, her mind whirling as she made her way to the abandoned adult cinema. By the time she slipped through the building's side door and headed towards the green room, the tension in her chest was almost unbearable. She forced herself to take a deep breath, pushing open the door to find Noah waiting for her, his usual cocky grin in place.

As they sat on the worn sofas, it wasn't long before the green room transformed into a pressure cooker of stress and unresolved tension. Blueprints and maps littered the coffee table like scattered remnants of some impossible puzzle, each potential entry point seeming more improbable and treacherous than the last.

"This is fucking impossible," Noah said, his frustration rising like a tide.

His fingers traced the intricate lines of a blueprint, pressing so hard that Chesney could see the muscles in his hand tensing. His face darkened, his jaw clenching so tightly it looked as though his teeth might crack under the pressure. His fists balled up, one slamming against the edge of the table hard enough to make it crack.

"Fuck!" he shouted.

Chesney tensed. She knew full well that a raised voice could carry beyond the walls of the abandoned cinema.

"Noah," she said sharply but with empathy, trying to cut through his rage. "You need to calm down. We can't afford to draw attention here."

"For fuck's sake," he snapped, a little quieter now, but still struggling to control himself.

The tension between them crackled like static electricity, threatening to ignite into something more volatile.

"We can't draw attention," Chesney repeated firmly, her fingers gripping her bat in sheer frustration. "Not here."

The statement was more than a tactical observation. It was a lifeline, a reminder of the stakes that hung over them.

Noah deflated slightly, the fight draining from his body like air from a punctured balloon.

"You're right," he acknowledged, a hint of his characteristic sardonic humour returning. "Fresh air?"

He jerked his thumb towards the exit, a gesture that was simultaneously an invitation and an escape.

"There's a takeout place nearby," he said. "We should take a walk and get something to eat."

Chesney's initial impulse was to refuse. Noah irritated her at the best of times and she didn't fancy sharing a meal with him. On this occasion, however, something deeper – perhaps the shared burden of their impossible mission, the unspoken understanding that they were both trapped in a scenario far larger and more complex than either of them could fully comprehend – made her reconsider.

"Fine," she said, the single word a complex negotiation of trust and necessity. "Lead the way."

Noah pushed open the creaky side door of the cinema, stepping out into the crisp night air. The city greeted them with its usual sound of distant sirens and the occasional rumble of a passing car. As they started walking, he glanced over his shoulder, a sly grin cutting across his face.

"There's a shortcut through here," he said, gesturing towards a narrow alleyway up ahead. "It's quicker, and it'll keep us out of sight."

Her muscles still aching from the previous night's marathon walk, Chesney nodded in agreement and then followed without protest behind Noah as he moved with a confident swagger.

As soon as they entered the alley, a flicker of movement caught Chesney's attention. There, in the corner of her vision, was the shadow again, with its disjointed, unnatural movement that didn't match the physical surroundings. It swayed and twisted as though it had a mind of its own, creeping along the walls with a fluidity that shouldn't have been possible.

I must be going mad, she told herself, frustrated.

She snapped her gaze away, focusing back on Noah, trying to shake off the odd sensation creeping up her spine. As they continued through the alley, Chesney did everything possible to keep her attention on the familiar rhythm of her steps and the crunch of gravel underfoot.

But then came the voice: soft and low, it slid into her mind like a whisper in the dark.

"Delgado is not to be trusted. He's a demon. He'll use you until you're no longer useful, and then discard you like the rest – that's if you even make it out from this job alive!"

Chesney's stomach dropped, her skin prickling with cold dread. She froze in her tracks, her heart pounding. Noah stopped beside her, his posture stiffening. His expression – wide-eyed with shock – told her everything she needed to know.

"What the fuck was that?!" he whispered shakily.

"You... you heard it as well?"

"Yeah, but not with my ears: with my head. Clear as day. What the fuck?!"

Chesney had no idea how to explain it. Her mind was spinning. They had both experienced the voice. It was impossible, absurd even, but it was happening.

She swallowed hard, trying to steady herself. The alley felt too narrow, too claustrophobic, and she could feel the panic rising again. She fought to keep it down, to stay calm, but the fear was real. She wasn't imagining things. This was real, this was tangible.

She didn't know what to say. She didn't know how to make sense of this. But one thing was clear: something far bigger than them was happening. Something that went beyond Delgado, beyond the job, and beyond anything they could understand.

It wasn't something they could ignore.

Chapter Ten

The cold night air hung heavy in the alley as Chesney and Noah stood rooted to the spot. Noah looked so rattled, more so than Chesney had ever seen him before, his usual cocky smirk replaced by wide, uncertain eyes and a furrowed brow. His hand hovered near his temple as if trying to massage the strange experience out of his mind, as though he feared speaking too loudly might summon the shadow again.

Chesney exhaled slowly, her breath visible in the chilled air.

"I... I've seen it before," she said, "and heard it too, just in my head. I'm kind of glad you have too; I was starting to think I was going crazy."

"I don't think this is the kind of situation

where "not going crazy" counts as a win," he said quietly, still shaken. "I'm not hungry anymore."

"Yeah," Chesney agreed. "Let's head back. We need to figure this out."

The green room was barely warmer than the alley, but at least it meant they could talk. Chesney dropped into her usual spot on the worn sofa, the springs creaking under her weight. She watched as Noah paced. He angrily kicked a discarded ball gag across the floor, causing it to roll unceremoniously towards the grimy wall. He was agitated, his usual swagger replaced by restless, jerky movements as if his body was struggling to burn off the shock.

"You said you'd seen it before," he said, finally stopping his pacing to lean against the arm of the sofa, his eyes narrowing at Chesney. "The shadow: what the hell is it?"

"I don't know," Chesney said honestly, "but it had the same weird movement, like it was alive. I even heard its voice in my head when I went to see Delgado in The Pit. Just like tonight, it warned me against him, saying that he was a demon. I mean, of course Delgado's ruthless – I don't need some weird intervention to tell me that. But this was different. Just like you heard tonight, the voice was so damn insistent, like it was desperate to warn me that this job we're on is a death sentence."

Noah's jaw tightened, and he looked away, his silence more telling than any words.

Chesney exhaled shakily.

"We could listen to it," she said. "Take the warning to heart, wherever it's from. But going against Delgado..."

She didn't need to finish the sentence. The consequences of betraying their boss didn't need spelling out.

"What do you think we should do?" Noah asked, a surprising vulnerability in his tone.

For a moment, Chesney was silent, struggling with the enormity of the situation.

"I think..." she said, pausing in disbelief at what she was about to say. "I think we need a second opinion."

Noah raised an eyebrow, waiting.

"Jade, my girlfriend," Chesney said, still afraid she was making a bad decision. "I would never normally do something like this, but she's good at seeing things clearly, even when everything feels like a mess."

Noah snorted doubtfully, the hint of his usual self creeping back in.

"You sure you wanna take this shit into your personal life?" he said. "It doesn't exactly feel like your style."

"It's not," Chesney admitted, pressing her lips into a thin line. "But you were there. She might not even believe me if I tell her about all this by myself."

The drive back to Chesney's apartment was quiet, except for the occasional clink of Noah's lighter as he lit a cigarette. The pungent scent of smoke filled the car, mingling with the faint, lingering smell of old fast food. Chesney stared out of the window, her mind whirling with thoughts of the shadow, the voice, and Delgado.

"Are you sure this is a good idea?" Noah asked, breaking the silence.

"It's the only idea I've got," Chesney said bluntly.

When they were a few blocks away from her apartment, Chesney instructed Noah to park the car.

"Pull over here," she said, gesturing to the curb. "We'll go through the alleys."

Noah rolled his eyes but still went along with it. The two of them quickly got out of the vehicle and then moved discreetly through the narrow passageways.

Chesney couldn't shake the discomfort of bringing Noah into her personal space. This wasn't a random hideout or meeting spot – it was her home. Her sanctuary. And yet, with everything spiralling out of control, she needed Jade's perspective.

She glanced at Noah as they neared her apartment building. Despite his obvious efforts to seem cool and unaffected, he looked as unsettled as she felt. His cigarette was long gone, his usual cockiness subdued. For once, he wasn't cracking jokes or making stupid comments. Chesney wasn't used to seeing him like this – quiet, thoughtful, and visibly rattled. Oddly, the fact that he shared her unease gave her a strange sense of camaraderie.

Chapter Eleven

The sound of the key in the lock seemed louder than usual as Chesney pushed the door open and stepped into the dimly lit apartment. She glanced back at Noah, who lingered awkwardly in the doorway.

"Come in," she said, still uncomfortable about bringing her work life into her home.

Noah stepped inside, his boots a dull thud against the mat. Chesney glanced at the clock on the wall. 2:12am. She sighed. She thought Jade might still be awake, though it wasn't guaranteed. Still, she decided to risk interrupting her sleep.

"Jade?" she called out. "I'm back! And we've got company."

A few moments passed in silence, during which Noah shuffled from foot to foot, looking strangely out of place without his usual bravado. The quiet stretched just long enough to feel uncomfortable before the sound of softer footsteps approached.

Jade appeared before them. Her hair was pulled into a loose bun, and she was wearing an oversized sweatshirt that made her look effortlessly cosy. Her eyes flicked from Chesney to Noah, taking in the scene with a patient curiosity.

"Hi," she said, stepping forward and extending a welcoming hand towards Noah. "I'm Jade."

Noah, to Chesney's surprise, straightened a little. His usual swagger was absent as he took Jade's hand.

"Noah," he said, calm and polite.

Even his voice lacked the snark that Chesney had half-expected. It was mildly astonishing to see Noah behaving like a pleasant human being. It made her wonder if she had perhaps underestimated him.

"Would you like something to eat? Something to drink?" Jade asked, her natural hospitality shining through.

"Uh, yeah. Thanks," Noah said, his voice softening even more.

Chesney gestured for Noah to take a seat on the couch in the living area. He sat down carefully, more respectful of this furniture than the scuffed-up chairs in hideouts – and even the battered seats of his own car. As Chesney watched Jade prepare something in the kitchenette, a part of her wished they could dive straight into the night's events, but the smell of something tantalising reminded her how long it had been since she'd eaten. Her stomach let out an audible rumble, and though she didn't comment, she saw Jade's lips twitch in amusement.

Jade returned a few minutes later with a tray of tea, toasted sandwiches, and a few snacks, setting it on the coffee table before taking a seat in the armchair.

"We need your opinion on something," Chesney began, now wasting no time, cutting through the otherwise relaxed atmosphere.

"This sounds serious," said Jade, raising an eyebrow.

"It is," said Chesney.

She took a deep breath and recounted everything: the shadow, the voice, its warning about Delgado and the job, the danger that seemed to be pressing closer with each passing moment.

By the time Chesney had finished, Jade's expression had shifted from mild curiosity to deep concern. She leaned back in her chair, processing.

"So... what do you think?" Chesney asked. "Do you believe us?"

Jade nodded slowly.

"I do," she said. "I've always believed there's more to this world than what we can see. And if what you're saying is true, it makes sense that someone – or something – might be trying to warn you."

Relief flooded through Chesney, loosening the knot of tension in her chest.

"Do you think the voice could be right?" she asked. "About Delgado being a demon?"

Jade tilted her head thoughtfully, a few strands of loose black hair falling into her face and framing her contemplative expression.

"Whether he's literally a demon or just acts like one, you could argue that there's not much of a difference," she finally answered. "Either way, he's dangerous. It takes a certain kind of evil to send people into situations where you treat their lives as being expendable."

"So what do we do?" Chesney asked Jade, exchanging a pointed glance with Noah.

Jade's gaze lingered on Chesney, then shifted to Noah. She took her time coming up with an answer.

"I don't think you should do the job," she said. "And honestly, I think you should stop working for Delgado entirely."

Chesney felt a spike of panic. As though she had forgotten it in her state of urgency for answers, it suddenly dawned on her that while Jade's advice was coming from a place of genuine care and wisdom, her girlfriend wasn't familiar with the brutal underworld in which they had to operate. Jade couldn't fully grasp the consequences of crossing someone like Delgado; she was lovely, sweet, and beautiful – qualities that made her so far removed from the darkness of the world. Chesney didn't want Jade to know this kind of fear, and she definitely didn't want her to live with the kind of worry that came from understanding what could happen if they crossed a man like Delgado. But Chesney also knew, deep down, that she couldn't leave things unsaid. To get Jade's best advice, she needed to be honest. Even if it meant revealing things that would make Jade afraid for her.

"Jade, you don't understand," she said. "And that's my fault. I hate the thought of causing you fear or worry, so I've always played it down. I've never even mentioned his name to you before tonight, but Delgado isn't the kind of guy you can just walk away from. He doesn't let things slide."

Noah, who had been quiet for most of the

conversation, finally spoke up:

"Look," he said. "Delgado isn't expecting an update for a few days. As far as he knows, we're still working on it. What if we just... lie low? Give it a couple of days and see if that voice shows up again."

"Seriously?" Chesney asked, not meaning to sound condescending, but cynical all the same. "You think we should just sit around and wait for some divine intervention to magically solve our problems?"

"It's not a bad idea, Chesney," Jade offered. "Lying low for a couple of days won't make things worse, and it will give you some time to think."

Jade's logic was hard to argue with. Chesney sighed and nodded.

"You can crash here tonight if you want," Jade offered to Noah, gesturing at the couch.

Chesney hesitated, but decided not to argue. Jade's kindness was one of the many things she loved about her, and there was no harm in having Noah stay close.

As Noah stretched out on the couch, Chesney followed Jade into their bedroom. The door clicked shut, leaving the strange events of the night temporarily on the other side.

Chapter Twelve

The aroma of sizzling garlic and herbs filled the small apartment, mingling with the rhythmic chop of Jade's knife against the cutting board. Chesney leaned against the counter, her arms folded as she watched Jade work. Noah lounged on the couch, scrolling idly on his phone, still looking slightly out of place in their domestic space.

"I'll admit it," said Chesney, "it's going to feel weird lying low like this. I'm used to keeping busy, not... waiting around for the sky to fall."

Jade glanced up from the stovetop, her expression calm.

"Maybe the downtime will do you some good," she said. "You can rest and think clearly."

"I'm just grateful for the food and a couch to crash on," Noah said, looking up from his phone. "Thanks again."

"You're welcome here, Noah," Jade said graciously.

Chesney rolled her eyes, but not unkindly.

"Don't make him too comfortable, Jade, or he'll never leave."

As they all chuckled, Jade began plating the food: hearty bowls of pasta with a fragrant, creamy sauce. Chesney's stomach grumbled audibly at the sight.

They gathered around the coffee table in the living area, bowls in hand. Just as Chesney was about to take her first bite, her phone buzzed loudly from its spot on the armrest. Frowning, she picked it up and read the message.

The text was from Mikey:

Something big has gone down at The Pit. You and Noah need to get here ASAP. Don't tell anyone.

"What's wrong?" Jade asked immediately, her tone sharp with concern.

Chesney didn't reply right away. Before she could respond, Noah's phone buzzed. He pulled it from his pocket, his eyes narrowing as he read the screen. He then turned it around to show Chesney. It was exactly the same message.

"We'd better go," Chesney said, sighing heavily as she set her bowl down. "Something's happened."

Jade's brow furrowed with concern, but she gave a small nod of understanding.

"It must be urgent," she said. "I won't press for details; now isn't the time. Just be careful out there, ok?"

Her eyes lingered on Chesney's, a plea for her to stay safe. Chesney, already on her feet, bent forward and gave her girlfriend a firm kiss on the cheek.

"Thank you," she said. "I'll explain everything later."

Chesney barely registered the rushed bites of food she took in between grabbing her bat from its usual spot by the door and shoving on her boots. Noah, already lacing up his own, managed a few hasty spoonfuls of dinner before they both threw on their jackets and stepped out of the apartment.

The night air was brisk, tinged with the faint smoky scent of the city. Chesney tightened her grip on her bat, holding it casually but with purpose as they moved beneath the glow of the streetlights. Around them, the city hummed with life – distant traffic, and music spilling out of restaurants and bars.

Chesney and Noah walked in tense silence, their breaths fogging in the cool air. Chesney's mind kept circling back to Mikey's text, the ominous words replaying in her head. Mikey wasn't the type to be careless – he was sharp, methodical, and always knew how to handle himself. He wouldn't have sent a message like that unless it was urgent, and the fact that it was so cryptic only made her stomach tighten further. She couldn't stop wondering what "something big" could mean. Mikey would have known the weight of those words. Sure, he could be loud at times, but he wasn't prone to drama or overreaction, which made the suddenness of his message even more jarring. Whatever it was, it had to be bad – bad enough that he had reached out to both her and Noah without even trying to sugar-coat it.

As they approached The Pit, Mikey was waiting for them outside. To a casual observer, he might have looked like just another guy loitering under the harsh glow of the streetlight, but Chesney could read him. The stiffness in his shoulders, the anxious tapping of his foot against the pavement – it all screamed worry.

"Something's bad," Chesney muttered under her breath.

Mikey spotted them and approached quickly, his movements controlled but urgent. His face, though set in a neutral mask, was pale enough to betray him.

"You're not gonna believe this," he said, his voice low. "Delgado's dead. Varga's crew hit the place earlier today."

"What?!" Noah exclaimed, though he kept

his voice a murmur. "You're fucking kidding?!"

"That's not even the craziest part," Mikey continued, glancing over his shoulder. "Come inside. You've gotta see it for yourself."

The interior of The Pit was barely recognisable. Tables and chairs lay overturned, shattered glass glittered on the sticky floor, and the walls were pockmarked with bullet holes. The air was heavy with the acrid stench of gunpowder and something far worse: a sulphuric tang that clung to the back of Chesney's throat.

And there, sprawled on the stage like a grotesque centrepiece, was Delgado's body.

Chesney felt her breath catch. The figure was unmistakably him – the same sharp suit, the same angular features – but his skin was a sickly grey, his hands clawed, his mouth stretched into an unnatural grimace that revealed jagged teeth. Horn-like protrusions jutted from his temples, and leathery wings lay crumpled beneath him.

Noah took a step back.

"Holy shit!" he blurted, forgetting to keep his voice low. "He really was a demon!"

Chesney felt sick, but she had to force herself to look away.

"We've seen enough," she said weakly. "Let's get out of here."

The three of them cautiously made their way out of The Pit, carefully weaving their way through the obstacle course of upturned tables as glass crunched beneath their boots.

As they stepped outside, the night felt jarringly calm. The air felt sharper now, cutting through Chesney's jacket and chilling her skin. No one said anything at first, the soundscape punctuated only by the distant hum of the city and the occasional clink of Noah's lighter as he flicked it open and shut without lighting a cigarette.

Instinctively, they knew they needed to put some distance between themselves and The Pit. Mikey took the lead, his wiry frame hunched slightly, his steps purposeful yet quiet as though he was trying to move unnoticed. Chesney walked beside Noah.

Mikey veered off the main street, leading them into a dimly lit alley a few blocks away. The narrow passage smelt faintly of damp concrete and stale rubbish, but it was just what they needed – far from prying eyes and ears. They needed to talk. Here, at least, they wouldn't be overheard.

Mikey finally came to a stop near a darkened corner, leaning against a graffiti-streaked wall. Noah leaned against the opposite wall, his usual bravado muted. Chesney stood between them, her arms crossed tightly, but the bat gripped firmly in one hand as if to shield herself from the implications of what they'd just witnessed.

"What now?" she asked, looking at Mikey.

"I'm gonna lie low for a while," he said firmly. "You two should do the same. It's likely that things will get worse before they get better."

Without waiting for a response, Mikey shifted his weight and glanced down the alley as if already planning his escape route. His posture was tense, his movements clipped, like a man who didn't want to linger long enough to let the conversation deepen. With a curt nod, he turned and disappeared into the shadows, leaving no room for further discussion.

Chesney and Noah exchanged a brief look before heading off themselves, walking several blocks in heavy silence. Eventually, they ducked into an alleyway to collect their thoughts.

"That voice was right," Chesney said quietly, her gaze distant. "Delgado was a demon."

Noah nodded, lighting a cigarette with shaky hands.

"Yeah," he said. "It makes you wonder what else it was right about."

Before Chesney could respond, the atmosphere in the alley seemed to shift. A soft ripple of energy pulsed through the air, like the faint hum of a distant storm, and a figure began to take shape before them. Chesney froze, her grip tightening on the bat as the alley seemed to shrink around her.

The transformation was almost imperceptible at first – a shimmer in the dim light, a flicker of motion where there had been none. Then, as if stepping through a veil between worlds, a woman materialised. Her arrival wasn't abrupt or jarring; it was seamless, almost elegant, as though the very air had woven her into existence.

The woman was striking: young – perhaps in her mid-twenties – with vivid red hair that caught the faintest light, glowing with a subtle radiance. It tumbled in loose waves around her shoulders, framing a face that was both alluring and defined. She wore a long black coat that clung to her form. Beneath it, hints of dark leather peeked out, adding an edge to her look, but still, taking her unusual arrival out of the equation, she didn't look strange at all. Her piercing green eyes locked onto Chesney with a quiet intensity.

For a moment, the alley felt uncomfortably still, as though the world itself was holding its breath. The energy that had rippled moments ago still hung thick in the air, buzzing faintly.

Chesney glanced at Noah, whose face was a mixture of confusion and alarm. He instinctively took a step back. She couldn't blame him; her own heart pounded erratically, and a chill crawled up her spine. She adjusted her hold on the bat, clenching it more firmly – a futile attempt to ground herself against the unsettling reality of what she was seeing.

The woman's gaze shifted between them, sharp but not hostile.

"Please don't be afraid," she said gently, raising her hands in a calming gesture, her posture open and non-threatening. "I'm Selena. The shadow you saw, the voice you heard: that was me."

Chesney stared at the woman, a flicker of realisation stirring within her. The voice that had echoed through her mind – strange, almost ethereal, like a distant song – was unmistakably the same as the woman's in front of her. Though it had sounded otherworldly when it had weaved its way through her thoughts, Chesney was certain that the essence of it – that timbre, that quiet but unwavering certainty – matched perfectly with the woman's voice. The link between the two was almost dizzying, but undeniable.

Chesney stood there, frozen for a long moment, unable to form a single word. Her mouth felt dry, making it hard to breathe comfortably, let alone speak. She exchanged a look with Noah, both of them wide-eyed and lost for words. They both looked back at the woman, too in awe, too shaken to do anything else.

"I'm a seer," Selena explained, seeming at ease, as if she had already prepared herself for the questions that would inevitably come. "I've been trying to protect you."

Her gaze met Chesney's and Noah's, a flicker of something that might have been sorrow in her eyes.

"I've been watching Delgado and Varga," Selena said. "I've been trying to prevent innocent lives from being caught in their mess. I'm not psychic, but in my shadow form, I can watch from a distance and see things that others can't: patterns, dangers, and people who need help. I've seen too many lives ruined by this stupid rivalry between Delgado and Varga. When I saw what the two of you were up against, I couldn't stand by and do nothing."

"Delgado's dead," said Chesney.

"I saw," Selena said. "Delgado didn't stand a chance against the number of people Varga sent. Still though, that's the price of the game Delgado chose to play. I suspect that sooner or later, Varga will probably face a similar fate."

"Is Varga a demon?" Chesney asked.

"Yes," Selena said confidently. "I've seen it for myself. That's demons for you. They are masters of deception and façade, but behind closed doors, I've seen it all. As soon as they shed their human mask, the reality of what they truly are becomes as clear as day."

"Wow," Noah uttered, the word tumbling from his lips.

"The tension between Delgado and Varga..." Selena continued. "From what I could see, it was getting more heated by the day. It was clear to me that things were only going to get worse. Their rivalry was going to escalate. It was only a matter of time before someone crossed a line that couldn't be undone. It was inevitable, really. But what wasn't inevitable was the collateral damage. People like you – people who have no true investment in these stupid rivalries – deserve better than to be put in potentially fatal situations."

Chesney felt the words settle in her gut, as if she had just been reminded of a truth she had buried deep down. She hadn't actively chosen this life. The life of an enforcer, of carrying out dirty jobs for someone like Delgado: she had stumbled upon it and fallen into it because it had felt convenient at the time. She swallowed a lump in her throat, thinking back to what Jade had said to her about how she could do anything she wanted – how she didn't have to settle for this kind of dangerous work. Jade had always believed in her, had always told her that she was capable of more, that she deserved better than being immersed in a world where the lines between right and wrong were blurred. And now, here was a seer, a woman who had witnessed everything, telling her exactly the same thing. It made Chesney feel guilty to think that she had been so willing to dismiss her girlfriend's words of support: not only were they kind and well-meaning, but most likely true.

"Why us?" Chesney asked Selena. "Delgado had lots of people working for him, and so does Varga."

"I could see you two were different compared to a lot of the people working for Delgado," Selena said, her voice quiet but firm. "You feel lost, yes, but you still have a chance to find your way out. I've been trying to protect those who still have a chance to choose a different path, to walk away from this mess before it consumes them."

Chesney's mind raced, trying to digest the enormity of what Selena was saying. This woman wasn't just some observer in the shadows; she was a force, a protector in her own right, someone who had seen the danger closing in on them.

Noah breathed out slowly, the confusion in his expression making it clear that he was still trying to process everything.

"So what now?" he asked, his voice controlled but full of uncertainty. "What do we do next?"

"In the grand scheme of things, that's up to

you," Selena said simply. "For now though, I hope that you'll both come with me."

Without waiting, Selena turned and began walking. After a brief hesitation, Chesney and Noah followed.

Chapter Thirteen

The air was crisp as Chesney followed Selena out of the alleyway, her boots tapping faintly against the cracked pavement. Noah trailed slightly behind, his hands shoved deep into his jacket pockets, the glow of the cigarette in his mouth casting a faint ember against the darkness. Above, the sky was a dull grey-black, clouds smothering any hint of moonlight, but the streetlights glowed in faint halos, illuminating their path.

Chesney's grip on her bat loosened slightly as they walked. Something about Selena's presence – calm, steady, unhurried – set her at ease. The tension in her shoulders hadn't completely melted away, but it was starting to dissipate. After everything Selena had said and done for them, Chesney's gut told her that they weren't being led into anything sinister.

"Where are we going?" Noah asked, his voice low but clear, breaking the silence between them.

"Somewhere you don't have to be afraid," Selena replied. "Somewhere you don't have to keep looking over your shoulder."

"And where exactly is that?" Noah pressed, still unsure.

"Through the city," Selena answered, her gaze fixed ahead. "Just a walk. A simple walk, without fear."

Chesney frowned, confused. It seemed too straightforward, too easy. But the sincerity in Selena's voice was disarming. Chesney couldn't help but wonder if this was Selena's way of making a point: a symbolic act of taking back a city that felt so thoroughly stolen by violence, danger, and demons – both literal and otherwise.

After a moment, Chesney found herself asking the question that had been burning in the back of her mind since they'd left The Pit:

"Selena," she started carefully, "do you think Varga will come after us? I mean... Delgado wanted us to plant an explosive in his territory. If he finds out we were involved..."

"He won't," Selena interrupted, her voice firm yet comforting. "From what I've seen, Varga doesn't know anything about what Delgado was planning. And even if he did..." She paused, glancing back at Chesney and Noah. "No offence, but Varga's got bigger fish to fry. He wouldn't be interested in chasing after a couple of small-time enforcers."

Chesney let out a breath she hadn't realised she'd been holding. Relief washed over her, lightening the heaviness in her chest. The impossible weight of Delgado's job had loomed over her like a storm cloud. The task had felt suicidal from the start, and now, suddenly, it was gone. The threat, the danger, the stress. All gone.

Her thoughts drifted to Jade and her kind words of wisdom: *You don't have to settle for this kind of work. You can do so much better.* Perhaps she had been right all along.

They walked in relative silence for a while longer, until Chesney noticed their surroundings starting to shift. She glanced at Noah, whose brow furrowed as he seemed to realise the same thing.

"Wait," he said, addressing Selena. "Are we heading to my car?"

Selena gave him a small, knowing smile.

"Yes," she said. "I want to make sure you get in it and drive home safely."

Noah blinked, then chuckled under his breath.

"I didn't realise you were doubling as my babysitter tonight," he said, albeit not ungratefully.

"Think of it as a one-time courtesy," Selena replied smoothly.

When they reached the familiar block where Noah's car was parked, the saloon sat under a flickering streetlamp, looking just as battered and scuffed as the last time Chesney had seen it. Selena turned to face Noah, her expression softening but her tone remaining resolute.

"You've worked hard to build this tough-guy act," she said. "But you don't need it anymore. Let it go, Noah. Move on to something better."

For a moment, Noah looked like he might argue, his mouth opening slightly. But then he stopped and nodded.

"Yeah," he muttered self-consciously. "Yeah, maybe you're right."

As he climbed into his car, he lit another cigarette, but Chesney noticed the way he handled it. There was no flourish, no exaggerated flick of his lighter. He inhaled deeply, but without his usual bravado. It was subtle, but Chesney saw it for what it was: an acceptance of Selena's words. Maybe, just maybe, Noah would take her advice.

Chesney stood beside Selena, watching as the car's engine sputtered to life. For a moment, its low rumble filled the stillness around them. Then, Noah pulled away, his car rolling slowly down the street. The faint red glow of his taillights grew smaller and smaller before finally disappearing into the darkness, leaving the street eerily quiet once more.

"I might not see him again," Chesney said aloud, her voice tinged with an unexpected melancholy.

"How does that make you feel?" Selena asked,

tilting her head and studying Chesney.

"I think... I think I wish him well," Chesney admitted, as much to herself as to Selena. "He's not who I thought he was. Turns out, he's not such an idiot. He's just... trying to get by, like the rest of us."

Selena smiled faintly, her green eyes gleaming in the dim light.

"It's good to wish people well," she said, "even when their paths diverge from yours."

They began walking again, with Selena subtly choosing their route. The city around them started to shift once more, the dimly lit, run-down streets giving way to wider avenues lined with neat rows of lampposts. Storefronts sparkled with clean glass, and the faint hum of late-night diners and bars filled the air. This part of the city felt alive, but in a way that was more polished – a stark contrast to the chaos Chesney was used to.

Eventually, they stopped in front of a charity shop. It was dark inside, its interior faintly visible through the glass. Nearby streetlights and the city's ambient glow spilled across it, casting a weak, uneven light. The window display showcased a hodgepodge of second-hand treasures: mismatched mugs, old books, a stack of board games, and a few gently worn jackets hung on a rack. Chesney found herself drawn to the eclectic array, her gaze wandering over the items before landing back on Selena, who was watching her thoughtfully.

"Chesney," Selena said, nodding towards the bat in her hand. "You should donate it."

"What?!" Chesney said, caught off guard.

"Some kids could use it," Selena continued. "Picture it: a group of kids playing baseball on a sunny afternoon. Your bat could give them that."

Chesney hesitated, glancing down at the bat. The thought of parting with it felt strange, almost sacrilegious. The bat had become a part of her image as an enforcer, a symbol of the life she had carved out for herself – or, at least, the life she had been living until now.

Sensing the conflict within Chesney, Selena tilted her head slightly, her expression softening with understanding.

"You don't need it anymore," she said gently, her tone kind but insistent. "Delgado's gone. This is your chance to step away from that life, to leave all of this behind for something better."

After a long moment, Chesney nodded and crouched down beside the bin liner full of donations, cuddly toys and clothes spilling out from its top. She pulled it open a little wider, creating just enough space. Carefully, almost reverently, she slid the bat inside, nestling it among the soft fabrics. Taking a moment, she adjusted the liner, tugging the edges closed to conceal the bat, ensuring it would remain safe until morning.

Selena's gaze was warm, her smile tinged with pride.

"Come on," she said, her voice soft. "I'll walk you home."

Chesney looked at Selena, gratitude flooding her thoughts. For the first time in what felt like forever, she felt lighter, freer. Together, they turned and began walking, leaving the bat – and everything it symbolised – behind.

Chapter Fourteen

The walk back to Chesney's apartment building was a quiet one. Selena led the way, her stride purposeful but unhurried, as though savouring the stillness of the city at night. Chesney trailed slightly behind, her thoughts tangled in the events of the past few hours. The streets seemed different now, not as suffocating as they usually felt. It wasn't just the absence of immediate danger; it was the presence of Selena, steady and self-assured, as if nothing in this city could touch them.

When they reached Chesney's building, the realisation hit hard: this was where they would part ways. Chesney stopped, her fingers curling into the fabric of her jacket as she looked at Selena.

"This is it, isn't it?" Chesney asked, sounding more fragile than she'd intended.

Selena nodded, a merciful smile tugging at the corners of her mouth.

"Yeah," she said. "This is it."

"Thank you," Chesney said, her voice raw with emotion. "For everything."

Selena tilted her head slightly, her expression sincere.

"You've got this, Chesney," she said, her belief in her words coming through. "Look after yourself, ok? You've got someone waiting upstairs who cares about you. Make it count."

Chesney wanted to say more, but the words caught in her throat. Before she could untangle them, Selena turned and started walking away. Chesney stood rooted to the spot, watching as Selena disappeared into the shadows of the city, her figure growing smaller until it vanished entirely.

The night felt heavier without Selena there, but there was also a clarity in the solitude. Chesney turned and let herself into the building, her boots echoing softly against the worn linoleum floors as she made her way to the apartment.

Jade was on the couch when Chesney walked in, her laptop perched on her knees and a mug of tea beside her. She looked up, her expression shifting instantly from neutral to concern.

"Are you ok?" Jade asked, setting the laptop aside.

Chesney shrugged off her jacket and hung it on a hook near the door before making her way to the couch. She sat down next to Jade, her movements slower than usual as she settled into the cushions. Placing her hands in her lap, she rubbed them together absentmindedly, trying to calm the rush of thoughts that had been swirling since she'd left the street.

"I've got a lot to tell you," she began.

Chesney started with Delgado – about how his rival had had him killed. She recalled the eerie moment when she'd seen Delgado's body, dead on the stage of his own nightclub, revealing his true identity as a demon. She described the encounter with Selena, and how, despite her initial doubts, Selena had guided her and Noah to safety. And then there was the part about Selena that still felt surreal: that she was a seer. She talked about how Selena was responsible for the strange shadows she and Noah had seen, and the voice they had both heard in their heads. She explained how Selena had gone above and beyond to warn them of the danger they were in. She described the walk through the city, Noah's departure, and finally, Selena's parting words.

By the time Chesney had finished, she figured that Jade's tea must have gone cold, but still her girlfriend hadn't moved once, her attention fixed as though hanging on every word.

After taking a slow, deep breath to steady herself, Jade leaned forward, her eyes searching Chesney's face.

"And what now?" she asked calmly. "What are you going to do?"

Chesney fiddled with the hem of her sleeve, her fingers twisting around a loose thread as she gathered her thoughts.

"I'm done," she said, looking Jade straight in

the eye. "No more enforcer jobs, no more running around in the shadows for people like Delgado. I'm done with all of it."

"Good. That's really good, Chesney," Jade said, her relief palpable, her shoulders relaxing as a smile broke across her face. "But... would it help if we moved? To another city, I mean. I'm just thinking that maybe it would give you that extra bit of help."

"What do you mean?" Chesney asked, frowning.

"This city..." she said, shifting her weight on the couch. "It's full of memories for you – and not good ones. Every street corner, every alley, there's something to remind you of what you've been through. Even if you're not in danger anymore, staying here might make it harder to properly move on."

"You really think we should move? Just like that?"

"Yes," Jade said with certainty. "I don't see any reason why we shouldn't. A fresh start would do you good. A new city, where nobody knows you as Delgado's enforcer or anything like that. I know you operated discreetly in that role, but you don't want to be constantly wondering whether someone will recognise you. You could start over. Find a job you actually want to do, make new memories."

"But what about you?" Chesney asked. "Wouldn't moving be a huge hassle?"

Jade laughed lightly.

"Not at all," she said. "A lot of my clients are online, and the ones who aren't... well, I could use the excuse to pare down my workload. Besides, I want what's best for you. If moving helps you heal and figure out what's next, then I'm all in."

Chesney stared at Jade, a blend of gratitude and disbelief almost overwhelming her.

"I've wanted you to get out of that life for a long time," Jade added. "If moving makes it easier for you to stay out, then it'll be worth it. Plus, I think it'll be good for you to be somewhere you can walk into a job interview without worrying about someone recognising you."

Chesney felt something shift inside, a sense of possibility she hadn't dared let herself feel before. She reached out, taking Jade's hand.

"Thank you," she said gratefully.

"You don't have to thank me," Jade replied, smiling warmly as she squeezed Chesney's hand. "We're in this together."

There was a tender silence between them, an unspoken understanding passing through the air. Their eyes met, and for a moment, it felt as if everything – every hardship, every fear – had led them here, to this quiet connection. The enormity of their shared experiences hung between them, but in that moment, they were just two people, finding solace in each other's presence.

"How about we get settled in bed?" Jade suggested, her tone gentle. "We can cuddle, just to unwind. No need for anything else, just... a bit of comfort."

***

Later that night, as Chesney lay in Jade's arms under the duvet, she felt an unfamiliar lightness. For the first time in years, there was no looming threat, no job to dread, no dangerous figure pulling the strings in her life. Delgado was gone. Selena had shown her a way out, and Jade was ready to help her build a new life.

It wasn't just an ending – it was a beginning. As Chesney closed her eyes, she let herself look forward to the future.